Where's Burgess?

Where's Burgess?

Laurie Elmquist

Illustrated by David Parkins

ORCA BOOK PUBLISHERS

Library and Archives Canada Cataloguing in Publication

Elmquist, Laurie, author
Where's Burgess? / Laurie Elmquist ; illustrated by David Parkins.
(Orca echoes)

Issued in print and electronic formats.
ISBN 978-1-4598-1478-3 (softcover).—ISBN 978-1-4598-1479-0 (PDF).—
ISBN 978-1-4598-1480-6 (EPUB)

I. Parkins, David, illustrator II. Title. III. Title: Where is Burgess?.

IV. Series: Orca echoes
PS8609.L574W54 2018 jC813'.6 C2017-904532-6
C2017-904533-4

First published in the United States, 2018
Library of Congress Control Number: 2017949695

Summary: In this early chapter book, a young boy deals with his parents' separation by focusing on finding his lost frog.

Orca Book Publishers gratefully acknowledges the support for its publishing programs provided by the following agencies: the Government of Canada through the Canada Book Fund and the Canada Council for the Arts, and the Province of British Columbia through the BC Arts Council and the Book Publishing Tax Credit.

Edited by Liz Kemp
Cover artwork and interior illustrations by David Parkins
Author photo by Ryan Rock

ORCA BOOK PUBLISHERS
www.orcabook.com

Printed and bound in Canada.

21 20 19 18 • 4 3 2 1

To Clay

Chapter One

He went missing on a Tuesday. I've made a poster. *LOST FROG. Answers to Burgess. Might be scared. BIG reward.* I've written our phone number in red letters.

"It doesn't even look like him," says my sister, Hazel, staring at the picture. She's twelve, and I'm nine.

"It does," I say.

"Are those teeth?" she asks.

"Yeah."

"And eyebrows?"

"Yeah."

She flips her hair off her shoulders. "Most people put up a photo."

"I need to get their attention," I say.

Mom slides a piece of toast in front of me. "I'll photocopy it at work," she says. "You can put the posters up after school."

"Paper?" says my sister. "What about the trees?"

Mom sighs. "This one time."

Mom works in recycling. Dad says she's on a mission to get everyone to reduce their trash for a whole year to an amount that will fit in a zip-lock sandwich bag. He says most people can't do it. He says he couldn't do it. He had too much garbage for Mom to handle. He lives in another city now. I look down at my toast slathered with peanut butter, the way I like it. I push it away.

"I'll eat it," says Hazel, taking the toast and biting into it. Her teeth grind away, and peanut butter smears the side of her cheek. “I’m sure we’ll find him,” she says. “How far can he go?”

“He might have caught a ride,” I say, pushing my chair back.

She shakes her head slowly back and forth. “Sometimes I wonder about you.”

She’s okay for an older sister because she likes to ride bikes and go places together. But we don’t always see the same things even if we’re standing right beside each other looking at them. She sees a frog. I see Burgess and everything he’s capable of.

“Everybody ready?” asks my mom, picking up her computer bag. “Teeth brushed? Reece, do you have your math homework?”

I grab my multiplication sheet and stuff it in my pack. I follow them out to our VW bus. *Burgess is out there alone. How can they act like nothing has happened?*

In class I draw a few more posters while the teacher reads to us. I draw Burgess with a suitcase under his arm. I give him shoes.

After school I put up the posters. I press the tacks deep into a wooden telephone pole. I smooth the paper down with my hand. It makes the pole look better to have something on it. People like to look at something while they're waiting for the bell to ring. I know I do.

I bend down to tie my shoelace. A shadow falls over me. "Are you that kid looking for his lost frog?"

I tie my lace into a knot so tight it cuts off the blood supply to my foot. Then I slowly look up.

"Yeah, that's me," I say.

He's the guy who got suspended for bullying. He's looking mean today. He cracks his knuckles, all of them at once, like a fist. He steps real close. His breath smells like a buffalo's butt.

"Who cares about a frog?" he sneers.

I don't know what to say. I can feel my brain jumping around in my head, trying to find the right answer. "They're pretty important, ecologically speaking," I tell him. "If frogs disappear from an area, the whole ecosystem can suffer."

He snorts. "It's probably flattened on the road."

"Maybe not," I say, but the image sticks in my head. Burgess squashed, and no one around to give him a decent burial. My stomach feels like someone just kicked it.

"Maybe somebody used it for bait," he says. "Stuck a hook in its guts."

A voice behind me says, "You wouldn't say that if it was *your* frog."

I turn around. It's Aaron, the kid who got the bully suspended. He wears a plush dark-blue bathrobe over his clothes. My stomach sinks. I might have been able to get out of this alive, but now I'm not so sure.

Aaron stands up on his toes. "Maybe someone should stick a hook in *your* guts."

I don't know why Aaron's picked today to be brave. But then I see the look of terror in his eyes, and I realize he's going to fall apart at any second. He grabs my arm. "RUN!" he screams.

Only I can't.

The guy's hand clamps my shoulder. His other hand curls into a fist and swings back. I close my eyes, waiting for the punch.

"Hey! What do you think you're doing?"

I open my eyes. It's Hazel—she's dropped her bike and run over. She whips her helmet off and throws it on the ground. Her face is all red, and her hair is frizzed out.

"Get your hands off my brother," she roars in his face.

The guy is so surprised, he lets go of my arm.

"You want to fight me?" she says, pushing up her sleeves. She is just as tall as he is. Her arms are strong from playing water polo.

He takes a few steps backward and spits on the ground. "It's not worth my time," he mutters.

Hazel takes a few steps toward him, but I grab her arm. "You're supposed to walk away."

"Tell that to *him*," she says.

He storms off as if he has better things to do. At the corner he gets into a red car that spins its wheels and churns up a lot of dust. "Morons," says my sister. She picks up her bike helmet and turns to me. "What was all that about?"

"Nothing," I say.

She stares at Aaron. "Why are you wearing a bathrobe?"

He shrugs.

"It's his thing," I say.

"Well, it draws attention," she says. "It means Neanderthals will pick a fight with you."

"I know," he says.

"It wasn't him," I say. "It was my frog posters."

She pushes her bike beside me down the sidewalk. "The two of you are ridiculous. I can't protect you all the time. I can't always be around. You should grow up. Nine is too old for this stuff. *Drawing pictures of frogs.*" She sounds mad, really mad, as she rides ahead of us.

Aaron looks at me. "I don't have a sister, but if I did, I'd want her to be just like yours. A barracuda."

Chapter Two

I have my father's staple gun. Mom says it's okay if I go around the neighborhood and put up posters. I can go to the end of the block and back. I have my phone with me. "Twenty minutes tops, Mister," says Mom.

Two doors down is a pole painted with vines and sunflowers. I bang up a poster of Burgess.

"What's this?" asks our neighbor. He's out walking his dog, a big brown Lab. On top of the dog's head is a Band-Aid with hearts on it. I've never seen a dog wearing a Band-Aid before.

"It's Burgess," I say.

"Where did you last see him?" he asks.

"In the backyard."

He looks up and scans the sky. "Lots of eagles around. At the beach the other day, one of them scooped up some dog's squeaky toy. Must have looked like something good to eat from way up there."

"He's a freshwater frog."

"Oh," he says.

"They don't swim in salt water, so they don't go down to the ocean."

LOST
Answers
Might be
BIG

"Smart."

His face is grizzled with white hairs. He smells like pipe smoke. It curls around him like an invisible cloud. Frogs are sensitive to smells. I doubt Burgess would have gone to him for help.

At our feet, his dog is eating a big chunk of grass. He spits it up in a slobbery blob. "What happened to his head?" I ask, pointing to the Band-Aid.

"A crow got him," he says. "Swooped down and pecked his head like it was a pumpkin."

Now I understand why our neighbor is obsessed with birds. But I'm not worried about Burgess. He knows better than to pick a fight with a crow. "I have to get going," I say.

"I'll keep an eye out for him," my neighbor calls out.

I walk to the end of the block, a busy road with cars and buses. I can imagine a frog trying to get across the road. At night it would be quieter. I've seen deer at night. They walk really slowly out into the road, so cars will see them. Deer are smart. They're urban deer. Burgess is smart too, an urban frog.

My phone buzzes in my pocket. I turn back for home. Mom doesn't like it when I'm late. She says that she, Hazel and I are *all in this together*. The three of us have to look out for each other. I liked it when Dad was here. He was good at looking after us. Dad always kept a baseball bat under the bed in case of intruders. I keep it under my bed now.

I open the door.

"Any luck?" asks Mom.

"I put up all the posters," I say. "If a frog doesn't want to be found, he's good at blending in."

"We got a call," says Hazel.

"You did?" My heart tap-dances in my chest.

"Don't get too excited," says Mom. "It was a false alarm."

"Someone thought Lost Frog was a band," says my sister. "They wanted to see if you'd play at their grad party."

"A band?" I ask.

"Yeah, they thought it was some sort of really cool promotion." My sister is standing at the stove, stirring a pot of milk. She's crumbling cheese into it, and I realize she's making my favorite, macaroni and cheese.

My stomach rumbles.

“Burgess isn’t a band,” I say, slumping at the kitchen table. “He’s my best friend.”

The kitchen fills with silence for a few seconds. It’s never silent around my sister and my mom. I look up. Mom’s eyes are red like they were when Dad left. They were red for a long time. I don’t want her to be sad.

"I'm starving," I say.

"Yeah, well, that's why I'm making dinner," says Hazel. "Mom says we can eat in front of the television and put something on Netflix."

Mom's blowing her nose.

"Yeah," I say, "that would be awesome."

Hazel looks at me and smiles. The real deal, where it reaches her eyes and they crinkle up and disappear. Somehow I've said something right.

Saturday morning, Mom leaves more posters for me on the kitchen table. I ask Hazel if she wants to ride over to the school playground. It's five blocks from our house, and I can't go if she doesn't come with me.

"I suppose," she says.

At the playground she puts her bike down under a tree and takes out her phone. She waves me away as if I'm a fly. I head to the other side of the school, over to the parking lot, where I haven't put up any posters yet.

When I turn the corner I see Aaron pushing his bike. I holler over to him, "Hey!"

He looks up, startled. We usually only see each other in class. We're not exactly buddies or anything. I walk over to him. "Whatcha doing?"

"Nothing," he says.

"Where are you going?" I ask.

"Nowhere."

Sometimes there are lessons at school on the weekends. Karate. But he doesn't look as if he's going inside. He's wearing a red-checkered bathrobe today. Flannel. He's just standing there, gripping the handles on his bike. Gripping them hard, white-knuckled.

"You want to put up some posters?" I wave the staple gun in his direction.

"Nah, I'm kind of busy," he says.

"Suit yourself."

He doesn't *look* busy. At school the other day, I thought that maybe he wanted to be friends. Guess I was wrong. I get on my bike and ride across the playground. I put up a few posters. *Whap! Whap!* I love the sound of the staple gun. I glance over to see what Aaron's doing.

He's on his bike. He's wobbly. He puts his feet down. Wobble, wobble, stop.

Wobble, wobble, stop. He looks like he just got his training wheels off. I laugh.

A car turns into the parking lot.

Aaron falls over.

Just like that. He's on the ground, and the bike is on top of him. The man in the car comes flying out the door and runs over to him. The man is bald. He's got his hand on Aaron's shoulder, and he's pointing to his car like he's offering him a ride.

Stranger danger. My arms are tingling like they do when you hit your funny bone. I spin my bike around and pedal hard back to him.

"Don't get in the car!" I yell.

They look up as I skid to a stop.

"This your friend?" asks the bald man.

"Yeah," says Aaron.

"We go to this school, and our moms know where we are," I say, getting between him and Aaron.

"I was just telling your friend that I have a first-aid kit in my car."

Aaron rubs his elbow.

"You can leave now," I tell Mr. Baldie.

"Okay," he says. "I'm going inside now. I teach karate in the gym. Been teaching here for about five years. If you need anything, just holler."

I feel kind of stupid.

Aaron doesn't seem to notice. He's just looking at his sleeve where he ripped it.

"What happened?" I ask.

"I fell over," he says.

"What did you hit?"

"Nothing," he says. "I just fell over. I always fall over."

"You do?"

"Yeah, that's why I'm here. I'm trying to learn *not* to fall over."

"Oh," I say.

"My dad said I had to learn to ride a bike *or else*." His face crumples, and his eyes get watery. His elbow is bleeding.

"We can go to my house," I say. "My mom has antibacterial ointment."

"Nah," he says, sniffing. "I only had half an hour, and now it's up. My dad will be mad if I'm late."

"But you didn't learn how to ride yet." As soon I say it, I feel bad, because that's probably the last thing he wants to hear.

"I have to go now," he says, as if he's waiting for me to go first.

"Okay," I say, pushing my bike back to Hazel.

"See you later," he yells.

I wonder what it's like having a dad that's strict. I wonder what he thinks of Aaron's bathrobes. It doesn't quite fit. I thought Aaron came from a family of artists who let him do whatever he liked. It shows you can be in the same class and not really know anything about each other.

"You ready?" asks Hazel, getting up from her tree.

"Yeah," I say. Then I ask, "Do you miss Dad?"

"Of course," she says. "Kind of a random question. Why do you ask?"

"I don't know. Maybe if he was around more, we'd do things with him on a Saturday morning rather than hanging out here."

"It was your idea," she says.

"Yeah, I know," I say.

Chapter Three

Mom's extended my geographical boundary for putting up posters. The dog park is okay, but not the community gardens where teenagers drink alcohol in the bushes. I can go as far as the corner coffee shop, where there's a big board for community events, but then straight home.

I turn the corner. I hear a cat meowing from a rooftop. It's a big fluffy thing, gray fur that sticks out at all angles like it went through the rinse cycle. It teeters on the edge. It keeps yowling, as if it's in trouble. I look around to see if anyone is going to save it.

A car pulls up to the sidewalk. One of those tiny Smart cars. A woman jumps out. She has red toenails that gleam in the sunlight. She looks at the cat and then at me. "She does this all the time," she says.

"Oh," I say.

"Go inside," she yells at the cat.

The cat walks to the peak of the roof, looks down at us and yowls.

She turns to me. "She likes to be up high. It gives her a better view of things."

I hold out the poster. "Can you ask your cat if she's seen Burgess?"

She reads the poster and calls up, "Louise, have you seen a green frog?"

"Actually, he's brown," I say.

"Looks green in the picture," she says.

"It's a flashier color," I explain. "Gets people's attention."

The cat jumps down to the balcony railing and tiptoes along it, its gray tail swishing.

"I lost a pet once," says the woman.

"A cat?" I ask.

"My budgie. It escaped from its cage."

"Did you get it back?" I ask.

"There were sightings," she says. "People called to tell me they'd seen a white bird flying in and out of the grass along the beach road. It had taken up with a flock of sparrows."

"Was it scared?" I ask.

"Oh no," she says. "I'm sure it was having the time of its life. It was free, and it was summertime. The living was easy." She's looking in the distance as if she can see it, but there's only a crow sitting on a branch.

The cat yowls again.

"I'll call if I see your frog," she says, "but my guess is, he's gone to Beacon Hill Park. They've got quite a frog population in those ponds."

"Thanks," I say, "but I don't think he's there. Burgess doesn't like crowds."

"Oh," she says.

"I'll just keep looking."

"Good luck," she says. "If you love something, set it free."

"I'll keep that in mind," I say.

Walking along, I pass a little kid on a bike. He's got training wheels and one of those enormous helmets to protect his head if he falls. He hasn't got the hang of it yet, and he wobbles to one side. His dad rushes up and grabs his jacket. Steadies him. I think about Aaron and his bike problem. Maybe he can't balance. Maybe he has something wrong with him. When I had an ear infection last winter, my balance was all wonky. I tried to put on my shoes and I fell over. I was a disaster.

I wonder if Aaron feels like a disaster. Maybe he needs a doctor to look in his ears.

At school, the teacher hands out cards and asks us to draw ourselves as ninjas.

I draw myself in a crouching position, circles for kneecaps. I color a black bodysuit over my whole body, covering my head, arms and legs. Only my eyes show. I look over at Aaron. He sits across the room from me, his head bent. His tongue sticks out as he draws. I wonder if mine does that.

"Let's give our ninjas warrior names," says Miss Ross. On the board, she's drawn herself as a ninja holding a book. I don't think she's quite got the concept. She calls hers *Ninja Reader*.

I call mine *SPEED*.

I draw my sidekick. A frog, also in full-on ninja gear. He's got thick legs and can leap really far. I give him those lines that fly out behind him. Action lines, they're called.

Aaron comes over to my desk. We're not supposed to talk, so he points to my drawing and gives me a thumbs-up.

I write on a piece of paper, *DO YOUR EARS HURT?*

He gets a big wrinkle in his forehead, like he's trying to figure out what I'm talking about. "No," he whispers. "Do yours?"

I try again. *EAR INFECTION = NO BALANCE = FALL OFF BIKE*

He nods slowly to show me he understands. Then he walks to the bookshelf at the back of the classroom, picks out a big heavy book and puts it on top of his head. Today, he's wearing his blue bathrobe, his favorite one.

He floats across the room with the book on his head.

A few kids laugh.

When he gets to his desk, he nods. The book slides down his forehead and into his hands. He cracks it open and starts reading.

So he has good balance. What, then?

That night I call Dad. He's in Vancouver, a long ferry ride from where we live in Victoria. "Are you coming to visit soon?" I ask.

"Fire season is starting," he says.

It means he's going to be in the forest for a long time. I'm not going to be able to call him. He'll be putting out fires and chopping down trees. Sometimes they even have to start fires before they can put them out. It's a strange business.

"I still haven't found Burgess," I tell him.

"Sorry, buddy," he says. "Your mom told me."

"Yeah," I say.

"I can get you another frog," he says. "We could get it from a pet store. They've got some really wild ones. I think we could even get you one that's blue."

"It wouldn't be Burgess."

"No, I know that. But your mom says you've been looking for a long time. She's starting to get worried about you."

"I still might find him."

"Yeah, that's true," he says.

"Dad?"

"Yeah?"

"I just wanted to hear your voice."

"Okay, buddy. You know I'm just making us some money, right? When fire season is over, I'll be able to visit more."

"Yeah, I know."

That night when I'm lying in bed, I hear Burgess. I know it's him. I fly to my bedroom window and listen real hard. It's dark, and there's a big round moon in the sky. I hear a cat yowling. I hear the neighbor next door rolling out his garbage cans. I don't hear Burgess again. But I know he's out there.

Chapter Four

Watching my mom ride her exercise bike gives me an idea. So far, all Aaron can do is fall over when he takes both feet off the ground. What if it is all about the feeling of pushing hard on the pedals? With an exercise bike, you can't fall over.

"Mom, can Aaron come over after school?"

Her T-shirt is sweaty under the armpits. She takes a swig from her water bottle. She pedals faster. "Aaron's a friend?"

"Yeah."

"Sure. He can stay for dinner, if you like."

"I don't know if we're that good of friends," I say. "It's kind of new."

"Whatever works for you."

"Can he ride your exercise bike?"

She wrinkles her forehead. "Does he want to ride it?"

"I think so," I say.

"As long as it's something he wants to do," she says.

Aaron slings his blue bathrobe over a chair. Without it, he looks skinny. He has freckles on his long arms. I try not to stare at them, but sometimes when you tell yourself not to stare at something, it's like your eyes have magnets in them.

I adjust the seat and push a few buttons. I set the level on four. He climbs on. "Just pedal," I tell him. "Hard."

"What about music?" he asks.

I put on the television and flick it to the channels with music on them.

"Pump up the volume," he says.

I give him something dancy. Mom likes it because it gets her heart rate up. It seems to be working for him too. Aaron's knobby knees are pumping up and down.

"Do you have any water?" he asks. "I need to stay hydrated."

When I come back with a glass of water, he's going uphill. He's panting and pushing. He's sweating.

"I mean when you do the outdoor version," I say.

"I like the indoor version," he says. "No cars to worry about."

I didn't know he was worried about cars. Now I do. "Do you want to stay for dinner?" I ask.

He gets off the bike and puts on his bathrobe. "I have to go home."

"Oh," I say.

"But thanks," he says. "It felt good to *ride*."

"Anytime," I say.

"Tomorrow?" he asks. "If it's okay with you?"

I shrug. "Sure."

That night I lie in bed staring at the glow-in-the-dark stars on my ceiling. Usually I fall asleep before they fade, but not tonight. I'm thinking about Burgess and how it was this time last spring that we found him.

Dad and I were camping on Salt Spring Island. It was our annual trip, just us two. We took a tent, sleeping bags, wieners and beans. We wore the same clothes every day, stinking like the campfire. We hiked the trails. Dad said it was forests like these that made him proud to be a firefighter. We were walking along a creek, and Dad saw him first. *Little brown guy*, he said, pointing to him.

The frog's body blended in with the mud. He didn't move, even when I stood just a few inches away. I cupped my hands around him and picked him up. His belly was soft, and I felt his heart beating.

Can I take him home? I asked.

He paused. *If your mom was here, she'd probably remind us that we aren't supposed to take animals out of their natural habitat.*

Yeah, I said. *But I still want him.*

Hard to argue with that, he said.

I carried him back to the campsite and put him in our cooler. We gave him some rocks and water from a stream so he'd feel at home. It was our last night at camp. I knew I wasn't going to see my dad for a while. He had packed up all his things, and they were sitting in a truck outside our house. Mom and he were doing a trial separation. Not a divorce. I hated that word. *Divorce.* A trial meant they might get back together. After fire season.

That night Dad rubbed his hands together over the campfire. I poked my head out from the tent. We posed with Burgess for a selfie.

Those were some good times.

Chapter Five

The next morning, I tell Mom we need to go to Salt Spring Island. I put the map in front of her.

"This is Ruckle Park?" she asks.

"You've got it upside down," I say.

"Oh yeah," she says, turning it. "This is where you and Dad went camping last spring?"

"That's the trail," I say, pointing to the dotted line that goes along the coast.

"And that's the creek where we found Burgess. I think he's gone back there."

"And how exactly did he catch the ferry?" asks Hazel, her hands on her hips.

"Hush," says my mother, studying the map and chewing her lip.

"Maybe he hitchhiked," I say.

"With his thumb?" Hazel asks.

"Frogs return to their streams," I say. "It's a fact. They use their sense of smell."

Hazel throws her hands in the air. She thinks Mom should do something about my obsession. I heard them talking the other night, but Mom said I was just going through a phase. A phase is something you grow out of. Burgess is not a phase.

"Can we go, Mom?" I ask.

Mom looks at me like she's thinking hard. Her eyebrows get all close together, and she gets a wrinkle between them. "Okay," she says. "We'll go Saturday. We'll take the VW bus and camp. We'll take a good look around. But that's it, okay? If we don't find him, we have to let him go."

I get a warm feeling in my gut. I love Salt Spring Island. Now if only Dad could come too.

The ferry to Salt Spring takes thirty-five minutes, enough time for me to put up some posters on the boat. "Don't be long," says Mom, as I slide open the door of our bus.

In the latest poster, Burgess's eyes have red veins.

"Hey, man," says a guy with a guitar. "That's a rad picture."

"Thanks," I say.

"He looks freaked out," he says.

"He's been missing for a while."

"Rough," says the guy. "I could help pass the word on the island. I'm going to set up outside the liquor store. Lots of people go in and out."

I look at his beat-up guitar. "Does that thing work?"

"Yup," he says.

"We could write a song about him," I say.

He picks out a few chords. "How does this sound?"

I look around to see if the other passengers are listening. A few of them have turned and are looking at us. It's a good sign. No one is running the opposite way. “Okay,” I say. “You’re no Usher or anything, but you’ll do.”

I take out a pen, flip over a poster and start writing. In a few minutes I have it all written out for him. The chorus goes like this:

I like frogs, yes I do
Doo bee doo bee doo
Small brown frogs, yes I do
YES I DO.

He strums a few chords, bends his head over the guitar and the words come out—slower than I thought they would.

I look around. “Maybe a bit more up-tempo.”

He strums faster.

I slap my thigh. “That’s it.”

He sings the chorus twice and ends with one of those big flourishes. All the strings jangle on the *YES I DO!*

The passengers around us clap, and I know we've made an impression. A girl comes up and takes a selfie of the guitar player and her. She takes a photo of the poster. "I'll tweet it," she says.

"I have you guys on video," says her friend. "I'll YouTube it."

"Thanks," I say.

An announcement comes over the ferry speakers that we're pulling into the harbor. I need to get back to my vehicle.

"I've got to get going," I say to the guitar player.

"Hang in there, man," he says.

When I get back to the bus, Mom says, "I was going to send out a search party."

"Yeah," says Hazel. "We were ready to hire a private eye."

"For Burgess?"

"For you, knucklehead," says Mom, starting the bus. It backfires, and the sound ricochets off the metal sides of the ferry. The guy who is getting into his car in front of us jumps a mile. He turns around and gives us a dirty look.

"Can we please buy a new car soon?" asks my sister. "Something from this century?"

"Nothing wrong with the ol' bus," says Mom.

"We can't get something new," I say. "Burgess wouldn't recognize it."

"That's ridiculous," says my sister.

We drive off the ferry and take the winding road to Ruckle Park. On the way, my sister pulls out her phone.

"No phones," says Mom. "We're off the grid this weekend."

My sister groans.

"It's for a greater cause," I say.

She turns to Mom. "A normal car and a normal brother. That's all I ask for."

Chapter Six

Ruckle Park has campsites for tents, but it also has eight spots for RV campers or old buses like ours. These sites are close to the hiking trail where Dad and I always set up. I've never been camping before with Mom. I'm not sure she knows what to do.

"You have to hang up the tarp," I say. "Dad always does that first so if it rains, we can go underneath it."

"I don't think it's going to rain," says Mom.

"Dad says it always rains."

She rubs the corners of her eyes like she's tired. "It's not going to be exactly like it is with Dad."

"Yeah," says Hazel. "Mom has her own way of doing things."

"We cook under the tarp," I say. "It keeps the food dry."

Hazel goes inside and brings out the tent and the sack with the poles in it. She and I are going to sleep in the tent while Mom sleeps in the bus. "Why don't you put the poles together?" she asks. "You like that job, right?"

I look down at the ground. "We have to lay a tarp first."

I'm not sure they know very much about camping. I wish Dad were here to show them how it all goes together. Hazel hands me the poles, and I snap them into a straight line. She brings out both tarps. When I look around, Mom's gone inside the bus.

Hazel shakes out the tarp, and bark flies from its folds. "Is she coming out?" I ask.

"Later," says Hazel.

"When are we going to look for Burgess?" I ask.

"Tomorrow," she says. "I think Mom's had all she can handle today."

"I know how to make a Norwegian fire," I say, my toe nudging the fire pit. "You start with big logs first. You lay them tight, side by side. Then you pile on smaller ones, then sticks, then tiny shavings. Like a pyramid."

"Show me," she says. "We can make Mom a veggie dog."

And that's how we spend our first night looking for Burgess. *Not looking*. But I figure he knows we're around. He probably heard the bus pulling in. I crawl into my sleeping bag. My sister's in the tent beside me, reading on her phone. Not using it as a phone is okay. "I'll read to you," she says, not waiting for my answer.

She reads some goofy book about vampires, but I don't listen to the words. I listen to her voice. It rises and falls. In the background the frogs are singing. They're loud. They sound like a thousand frogs all singing the same song. They sound alive.

When I get up in the morning, Mom's already frying bacon on the Coleman

I'm the one who pays the bills.

And Dad?

Yeah, she said. *Him too.*

When I see the creek, I recognize it right away. It has a wooden bridge with some kind of steel grate on it so it's not slippery. I remember crossing it with Dad. I climb down through the ferns to the edge.

"Wait!" calls Mom.

But I'm already down the bank and yanking off my boots. The water is cool on my feet, and the rocks are slimy. I look for a brown frog. There are fish, and I even think I see something move, but it's an old rotting stick.

Hazel walks in too. "Burgess," she calls, "where are you?"

Even Mom, who can't swim and doesn't like cold water, comes into the creek. She's wearing those river shoes with rubber soles. She has a pole for balance. It's quiet in the creek except for my sister's voice, growing fainter as she walks downstream. "Yoo-hoo, frog! Yoo-hoooo, Burgess!"

"It's nice here," says Mom. "I can see why you like it."

"Yeah."

"It's a good place for a frog."

"Yeah."

"Even if we find him, would you want to take him back home?" she asks. "He did go to a lot of work to get here. What with the ferry and all. And the hitchhiking."

I know what she is saying, but I don't like letting go of him. It feels like there's a hole in my heart that will never fill. He was the last thing Dad gave me

I swallow hard. "It was better with Burgess, but yeah, it's not so bad."

Hazel is waiting on the bridge. "Are we ever going to get out of here?" she calls.

"I think we're ready," says Mom, getting up and pulling me with her.

Back at the harbor, we park with all the other cars and trucks waiting for the ferry to arrive. In the pickup in front of us, a guy is giving his dog a drink of water. It's a huge St. Bernard with a slobbery tongue.

"It says we have Wi-Fi here. Can I check my phone?" Hazel scrolls through all the messages she's missed while we we've been off the grid. She goes on the Internet. Then she squeals. "There's your poster," she says. "Look."

It's Burgess's bulging eyes and outspread arms.

"He's trending," she says. "He's been retweeted 1,739 times."

"It doesn't matter now," I say.

"But it means people care," says my mom. "That's something."

I lean back in my seat and stare out the window. Maybe she's right. Burgess was only a small brown frog, but he made an impression on people.

"There's a song," says my sister. "Some guy is singing about your frog."

"I know," I say.

"That's you," she says, then shows Mom the video. "There's Reece!"

Mom takes the phone. "It certainly is." We all listen to the song a few times. It's catchy, and my sister says the guitar player has nice hair.

Chapter Seven

Aaron's been riding the stationary bike every day after school. Mom says it's time we pushed him out of the nest. She is taking us to a paved bike trail where Aaron won't get mowed down by cars. Everyone rides this trail, even five-year-olds, so I think he'll be okay.

Mom unloads our bikes off the back of the bus. "So you want me to ride up ahead? Is that the plan?"

"Yes," says Aaron.

He doesn't want any adults around. He thinks all adults are as strict as his dad, although I tell him Mom is one of the good ones. Plus, he's eaten dinner a few times at our house now, so you'd think he'd be okay around her. But he's not. He gets jittery.

"We'll be fine," I say.

"I'll be just up ahead," she says. "Keep an eye out for cougars, and if you see one, make a lot of noise—"

"We got the lecture at school," says Aaron.

Sometimes he's rude. He doesn't mean to be. I've told him adults like a softer tone, and they don't like being interrupted. I've learned to count silently in my head while adults are talking.

It gives my face a look like I'm listening, which I am, but not with all my brain.

"We'll watch out for everything," I tell her.

Mom pecks me on the cheek, and I let her. Then she pedals off. She waves, and I wave back.

"You want to stop for lunch?" asks Aaron.

We haven't even started yet, but I don't mind. I'm kind of hungry anyway. We have egg-salad sandwiches in our packs. I can smell them. Mom makes the best sandwiches—about two inches thick.

We push our bikes to a place off to the side of the trail that has trees and a grassy spot that looks over the water. The sandwiches are still cool from the fridge.

Aaron stuffs it in his mouth and chews like he hasn't eaten in days. He swallows hard and smiles. "This is the life," he says.

"Yeah," I say, watching families cycle by.

A little girl with orange hair slows her bike and stares. Her dad is all spandexed-out like Spider-Man. "Eyes ahead, eyes ahead," he calls out. She pedals fast to keep up with him.

I turn to Aaron. "Does your dad ride?"

"Nah," he says.

"So why does he want *you* to?"

He looks down at his feet. "He says it's embarrassing to have a kid who can't ride a bike. Says everyone can do it."

A text comes in from Mom. **Where are you guys?**

I text her back. **Eating lunch.**

"You ready?" I ask, getting to my feet. There's no one on the trail around us.

Aaron's face looks white. "It's do or die."

"Do you want me to follow behind you?"

"No," he says. "I don't want anyone watching me."

"Do you have the theme song in your head?"

"Yup," he says, looking determined just like Rocky.

I get on my bike and shove ahead, pedaling. I don't look back. I give him his space. I count in my head backward from ten and then forward. He hasn't called out. I haven't heard a crash or anything.

Then I hear it. A whoosh and whizz and Aaron's beside me. I look over, but he's looking straight ahead. His smile is like one of those skull smiles, overly big, showing all the gums. A scared smile. But he hasn't fallen over. He's going fast, and I pedal hard to keep up with him.

He still doesn't look over, but he speaks. "You're right," he says. "If I pedal hard, I don't fall."

"Yeah," I say.

We're coming up to a family. They're walking with a stroller and a wiener dog on a long leash.

"From behind!" I yell.

They move to the right just in time for Aaron to go whizzing by.

"It's his first time," I yell to them.

Aaron laughs like a madman. His blue bathrobe flaps behind him.

He swerves and pedals like his life depends on it. Do or die. But he doesn't fall off. "Reece, do you see?" he yells. "Do you see me? I'm riding a bike."

I feel something shift in my chest like a lump. For the first time since losing Burgess, I feel really good. I realize I haven't thought about my lost frog in a few days. Aaron's up ahead. He waves to Mom, who has been waiting for us at the side of the trail.

"Look," he calls out to her. "I can do it."

"Bravo," she says, getting on her bike.

And we cycle down the trail, the three of us.

Acknowledgments

I'd like to acknowledge the support of my husband, Clay Elmquist, who was with me on Salt Spring Island when we saw a poster tacked to the ferry terminal message board. *LOST FROG. Answers to Burgess.* He said, "That would make a good story." Sometimes that's all a writer needs.

Thanks to my parents, Ernest and Judith Abel, for giving me Isaac Lake, Ontario, an amazing place to grow a writer's imagination. A big thanks to Jack and his *I Love Monkeys* song (Yes, I do!) that inspired Reece's song about his lost frog.

Thanks to my editors, Amy Collins and Liz Kemp, who championed the book and provided their editorial expertise, and to everyone at Orca Book Publishers. Special thanks to David Parkins for his drawings of Reece Hansen and Burgess the frog.

Laurie Elmquist holds an MA in Literature and Creative Writing from the University of Windsor in Ontario. She enjoys writing for kids, and is the author of *Beach Baby*, *Forest Baby* and *Where's Burgess?*, which was inspired by a *Lost Frog* poster she saw on a camping trip. Laurie teaches at Camosun College in Victoria, British Columbia, and is an online instructor at the University of Calgary in Alberta. For more information, visit www.laurieelmquist.com.

Check out the adventures of Cyrus and Rudy!

ORCA BOOK PUBLISHERS
www.orcabook.com

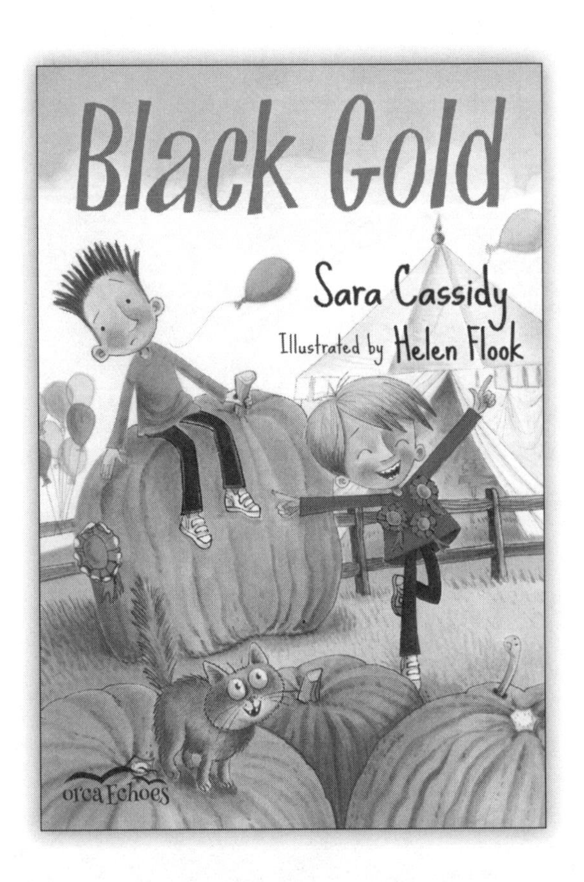

"Jam-packed with likable, well-realized characters."
-Kirkus Reviews